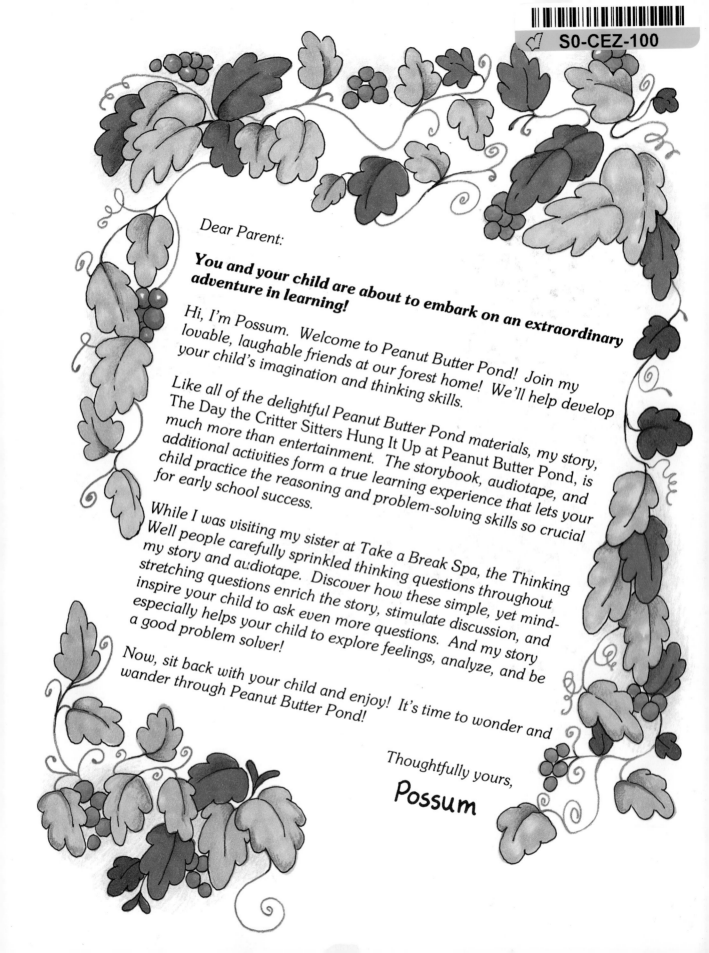

Dear Parent:

You and your child are about to embark on an extraordinary adventure in learning!

Hi, I'm Possum. Welcome to Peanut Butter Pond! Join my lovable, laughable friends at our forest home! We'll help develop your child's imagination and thinking skills.

Like all of the delightful Peanut Butter Pond materials, my story, The Day the Critter Sitters Hung It Up at Peanut Butter Pond, is much more than entertainment. The storybook, audiotape, and additional activities form a true learning experience that lets your child practice the reasoning and problem-solving skills so crucial for early school success.

While I was visiting my sister at Take a Break Spa, the Thinking Well people carefully sprinkled thinking questions throughout my story and audiotape. Discover how these simple, yet mind-stretching questions enrich the story, stimulate discussion, and inspire your child to ask even more questions. And my story especially helps your child to explore feelings, analyze, and be a good problem solver!

Now, sit back with your child and enjoy! It's time to wonder and wander through Peanut Butter Pond!

Thoughtfully yours,

Possum

ISBN 1-55999-146-1

A division of LinguiSystems, Inc.

Other products in the Peanut Butter Pond Series:

The Day Snake Saved Time	A001
The Day Porcupine Put On the Dog	A002
The Day Woodchuck Would Chuck Wood	A003
The Day They Smelled a Skunk	A108
The Day Bird Almost Flew the Coop	A107
My Peanut Butter Pond Think 'n' Do Book	A004
My Peanut Butter Pond Think-Along Funbook	A110
Peanut Butter Party: A Think 'n' Play Game	A005

Thinking Well
3100 4th Avenue
East Moline, IL 61244

1-800-U-2-THINK

The Day the Critter Sitters Hung It Up

at Peanut Butter Pond

Story by Lael Littke
Illustrated by Stephanie McFetridge Britt

Possum was like the old woman who lived in the shoe. She had so many children she didn't know what to do.

If Possum wasn't bathing her children, she was washing their clothes.

If she wasn't teaching them their ABC's, she was showing them how to poke under old logs to find juicy slugs and bugs.

What other things could Possum do with her children?

One day Woodchuck said, "You look tired, Possum. Why don't you take a day off?"

"I can't take a day off," Possum said. "Who would watch all these little tykes?" She pointed at her five babies.

Snake slithered away and hid in a log. Bird flew to the top of Tall Tree.

Woodchuck gazed at the little possums who sat quietly, watching their mother. "I can do it," he said with confidence. "Look how well they behave."

Beaver nodded. "I'll help, too. You really do need a little vacation, Possum."

Possum looked hopeful. "I'd enjoy going to visit my sister at the Take a Break Spa. But do you really think you can handle the children?"

Woodchuck smiled. "No problem. There are two of us, and we're smarter than they are."

Why do Woodchuck and Beaver think they're smarter than Possum's children?

"All right, I'll go, but just for one day," Possum said. "Are you sure you'll be okay?"

Woodchuck smiled at the children. "What could go wrong in just one day?"

Possum happily kissed the little possums good-bye, telling each one to obey Woodchuck and Beaver while she was gone.

Possum hurried away toward the Take a Break Spa. The little possums watched her disappear around the bend of the path. They all burst into tears. "Whah!" they howled. "Boo-hoo! Mama!"

Why are the possum babies crying?

All five little possums started up the path after their mother.

"Wait!" yelled Woodchuck. "Stay here! We're going to have a lot of fun together."

The little possums kept going.

"Ice cream!" Beaver yelled.

The little ones came running back.

Why did the little possums come back?

"Count them," Beaver said. "Are they all here?"

Woodchuck counted. "One – two – three – four – five. Yes, they're all here. But don't you think they should have lunch before they have ice cream?"

The little possums burst into tears again. "Whah!" they howled. "We want ice cream NOW!"

The possum babies kept crying until Woodchuck and Beaver took them to Peanut Butter Pond General Store and ordered five fish-flavored ice cream cones.

What flavor of ice cream would you order?

Pretty soon all five little possums smelled like herring and mackerel.
Ice cream covered their faces and dripped onto their clothes.

"Possum won't like this," Woodchuck said. "We'll have to give them
all a bath in the pond."

Beaver nodded. "That won't be hard. There are two of us, and we're
smarter than they are."

Woodchuck and Beaver popped each little possum into Peanut Butter Pond.

"Whee!" yelled the little possums. "Swimming!"

Why are the baby possums REALLY in Peanut Butter Pond?

"No, not swimming," Woodchuck said. "Baths."

"We hate baths!" the little possums yelled. They swam away from Woodchuck, splashing and diving. Woodchuck grabbed whoever came close to him and applied the soap. He got soapsuds in his eyes and couldn't tell which little possums he had cleaned and which ones he hadn't.

By the time he finished, Woodchuck figured he had bathed at least thirty little possums.

While Woodchuck was bathing the babies, Beaver washed their clothes and hung them up to dry. Then Beaver went to Possum's house and got nightshirts.

How would you give the little possums their baths?

Beaver put a nightshirt on each little possum as Woodchuck fished the possums out of the pond.

"Count them," Woodchuck said. "Are they all here?"

Beaver counted. "One – two – three – four – five. Yes, they're all here. And maybe the nightshirts will make them think about naps."

But the little possums didn't think about naps. "Play!" they yelled gleefully, running all around the clearing, their nightshirts flapping.

One little possum spied Snake sunning himself on a warm rock. "Jump rope!" the little possum yelled.

Why did the little possum yell "jump rope"?

Two little possums grabbed Snake. They turned him like a jump rope, whipping him against the dusty ground. The other little possums jumped over Snake. "Fun!" they yelled.

"Ssssomebody sssssave me!" gasped Snake.

Woodchuck and Beaver ran to rescue Snake.

How would you rescue Snake?

Woodchuck and Beaver pried Snake away from the little possums.

Snake examined his middle, which was stretched from hitting the ground so many times.

"How long has it been ssssince Possum left?" Snake sighed.

Woodchuck wiped his forehead with his handkerchief. "It seems like two years," he said wearily.

Snake slithered swiftly away to hide under a log.

The little possums scattered over the clearing. Two swung by their tails from the limbs of Tall Tree. Two wrestled in the dirt. One dove back into Peanut Butter Pond.

If Possum could see her children now, what would she say?

"We'll play tag!" Beaver whispered frantically.
"That will wear them out." He shouted to the little
possums, "Come and chase Uncle Beaver!"

Laughing, the little possums chased Beaver around the
clearing until he couldn't run any more.

Then the little possums chased Woodchuck until . . .

he couldn't take another step.

Do you think the Baby Possums are tired now? Why?

"Count them," Beaver said. "Are they all here?"

Woodchuck counted. "One – two – three – four – five. Yes, they're all here, but they're dirty again."

Beaver groaned. "We don't have any more clothes to put on them."

Woodchuck thought about it. "We'll just have to wash them in their nightshirts and hang them up to drip-dry."

So Woodchuck and Beaver dunked the little possums one by one in Peanut Butter Pond. Then they let them hang by their tails from the branches of Tall Tree.

Why don't the little possums mind hanging by their tails?

Woodchuck was so tired that he gave a big yawn as he hung up
the fourth little possum.

"I can yawn bigger than that," one little possum said.

"So can I," said another one.

Pretty soon the little possums were having a yawning contest.

What do you think will happen if the baby possums keep yawning?

Before the little possums knew it, they had yawned themselves to sleep.

Woodchuck sat down with a cold cloth on his head.

Beaver stretched out on the ground and closed his eyes.

And that's the way they were when Possum came back. She looked fondly at her sleeping children.

"I had such a lovely day," she whispered. "What can I do to thank you for watching all my children?"

"Give us your sister's address," Woodchuck said weakly. "We need a day at the Take a Break Spa."

Think 'n' Tell

What should Possum find out about her babysitters before she goes away for a day?

Would you like Woodchuck and Beaver to be your babysitters? Why?

How do you think Woodchuck and Beaver felt about their day with the little possums?

What would you do with the little possums if you were their babysitter? Why?

Mother Possum helped her babies write a thank-you note to Woodchuck and Beaver. What do you think the note said?

Hop Over the Pond

On hot summer days, the little possums take turns hopping over the pond. Sometimes the possums don't hop far enough. Then, splash! They fall into the pond and get wet. Play your own game of hop over the pond. But don't get wet!

What you need:

- construction paper
- crayons
- scissors
- string

What to do:

1. Draw three or four big fish shapes on construction paper. Then, cut them out.

2. Put two strings on the floor about 12" apart to make a pond.

3. Put the fish on the floor between the strings.

4. Hop over the pond.

5. After each successful hop over the pond, move the strings further apart. How far can you jump without falling into the pond?

How is the pond in this game like a real pond? How is it different?

Fruit Fingers

The possum family loves fruit, so while Mother Possum cooks dinner, the little possums make fruit fingers for dessert. Choose your favorite fruits. Then, make fruit fingers for your family's dessert.

What you need:

fruit — apples, oranges, grapes, bananas, etc.
bamboo skewers
index cards
crayons
serving tray

What to do:

Cut your favorite fruits into bite-sized pieces. Use your fingers to push one piece of fruit at a time onto a skewer. Be creative! Make a different fruit finger for each member of your family.

Draw a picture of each fruit finger on separate index cards. Arrange the fruit fingers on a serving tray. After dinner, give an index card to each person. Then, ask each person to find the dessert that matches his card.

Why do the little possums call this dessert fruit fingers?

Peanut Munch Race

Possum knew how to have fun with a bagful of unshelled peanuts. She sprinkled five paths with peanuts. Then, she let the little possums have a peanut munch race to Peanut Butter Pond.

What you need: unshelled peanuts

What to do:

1. Sprinkle unshelled peanuts along two paths to the finish line a few feet away. Use the same number of peanuts on each path.

2. At the signal, two players, one on each path, must crawl on their hands and knees, shelling and eating their peanuts as they go.

3. The first player to eat all his peanuts and cross the finish line wins.

Play the peanut munch race alone. Each time you play, try to reach the finish line faster than before.

Play the peanut munch race with your friends. Sprinkle unshelled peanuts along a separate path for each player.

When the peanut munch race is over, have another race. The first player to pick up the peanut shells left along her path wins!

Would you be full when you finish this race? Why?

Causin' Trouble, Havin' Fun!